YORK NOTES

The Long and the Short and the Tall

Willis Hall

Notes by Graeme Lloyd

The right of Graeme Lloyd to be identified as Author of this Work has been
asserted by him in accordance with the Copyright, Designs and Patents Act 1988

YORK PRESS
322 Old Brompton Road, London SW5 9JH

ADDISON WESLEY LONGMAN LIMITED
Edinburgh Gate, Harlow,
Essex CM20 2JE, United Kingdom
Associated companies, branches and representatives throughout the world

First published 1998

ISBN 0–582–36843–X

Designed by Vicki Pacey, Trojan Horse, London
Illustrated by Chris Brown
Phototypeset by Gem Graphics, Trenance, Mawgan Porth, Cornwall
Colour reproduction and film output by Spectrum Colour
Produced by Addison Wesley Longman China Limited, Hong Kong

CONTENTS

PREFACE

York Notes are designed to give you a broader perspective on works of literature studied at GCSE and equivalent levels. We have carried out extensive research into the needs of the modern literature student prior to publishing this new edition. Our research showed that no existing series fully met students' requirements. Rather than present a single authoritative approach, we have provided alternative viewpoints, empowering students to reach their own interpretations of the text. York Notes provide a close examination of the work and include biographical and historical background, summaries, glossaries, analyses of characters, themes, structure and language, cultural connections and literary terms.

If you look at the Contents page you will see the structure for the series. However, there's no need to read from the beginning to the end as you would with a novel, play, poem or short story. Use the Notes in the way that suits you. Our aim is to help you with your understanding of the work, not to dictate how you should learn.

York Notes are written by English teachers and examiners, with an expert knowledge of the subject. They show you how to succeed in coursework and examination assignments, guiding you through the text and offering practical advice. Questions and comments will extend, test and reinforce your knowledge. Attractive colour design and illustrations improve clarity and understanding, making these Notes easy to use and handy for quick reference.

York Notes are ideal for:
- Essay writing
- Exam preparation
- Class discussion

The author of these Notes is Graeme Lloyd. He is Head of English at a comprehensive school in County Durham and Examiner for a major examining board.

The text used in these Notes is the 1994 Heinemann edition edited by Maureen Blakesley.

Health Warning: **This study guide will enhance your understanding, but should not replace the reading of the original text and/or study in class.**

PART ONE

INTRODUCTION

HOW TO STUDY A PLAY

You have bought this book because you wanted to study a play on your own. This may supplement classwork.

- Drama is a special 'kind' of writing (the technical term is 'genre') because it needs a performance in the theatre to arrive at a full interpretation of its meaning. When reading a play you have to imagine how it should be performed; the words alone will not be sufficient. Think of gestures and movements.

- Drama is always about conflict of some sort (it may be below the surface). Identify the conflicts in the play and you will be close to identifying the large ideas or themes which bind all the parts together.

- Make careful notes on themes, characters, plot and any sub-plots of the play.

- Playwrights find non-realistic ways of allowing an audience to see into the minds and motives of their characters. The 'soliloquy', in which a character speaks directly to the audience, is one such device. Does the play you are studying have any such passages?

- Which characters do you like or dislike in the play? Why? Do your sympathies change as you see more of these characters?

- Think of the playwright writing the play. Why were these particular arrangements of events, these particular sets of characters and these particular speeches chosen?

Studying on your own requires self-discipline and a carefully thought-out work plan in order to be effective. Good luck.

Early years   Willis Hall was born in Leeds, England, in 1929. He spent his early life there before leaving school to join the army at the age of seventeen. He served with the army in the Far East for several years. As well as providing inspiration for *The Long and the Short and the Tall*, his time in the Far East gave him his first experience as a script-writer: working for Radio Malaya.

The play   *The Long and the Short and the Tall* is Hall's most successful play. It was first performed at the Nottingham Playhouse in September 1958, with Robert Shaw as Mitchem and Peter O'Toole as Bamforth. It won the *Evening Standard* Best Play of the Year award in the same year. However, despite this success and good reviews, the play only ran for three months in the West End, perhaps because its obvious ambivalence towards war was ahead of public opinion.

Since its first performance the play has been performed all over the world, frequently being adapted to fit other conflicts in other countries. It has even been performed in Japan where the members of the patrol were Japanese and the prisoner was a British soldier. The play has also been made into a film, for which Willis Hall wrote the screenplay.

Other work by the author   Willis Hall has had other major successes, particularly those written in collaboration with Keith Waterhouse, a friend from his early years. Most notable was the adaptation of Waterhouse's novel, *Billy Liar*, for the stage. Again, the play was made into a film for which the pair produced the screenplay. Other screenplays include *Whistle Down the Wind* and *A Kind of Loving*.

Willis Hall also writes extensively for television. *The Return of the Antelope*, a children's series for Granada television, has been broadcast in more than sixty countries.

CONTEXT & SETTING

Historical background

The Long and the Short and the Tall is set in the Malayan jungle early in 1942 at a time in the Second World War (1939–45) when the Japanese army was advancing towards the British-held base at Singapore. Because it was a port British commanders assumed the Japanese would attack from the sea and had therefore concentrated upon strengthening the city's marine defences. However, when the attack came it was by land down the Malayan Peninsula and the British were taken completely by surprise.

The British army in the Second World War

In peace time Britain maintained a relatively small army whose principal role was to safeguard the various outposts of the British Empire. It was this small professional army which Willis Hall joined at the age of seventeen. At the outbreak of the Second World War the introduction of conscription swelled the ranks of all the armed services with men who had been compelled to fight rather than those who chose to volunteer. In *The Long and the Short and the Tall* the two professional soldiers and the five conscripted men represent this new British army.

The dramatic impetus of the play is in part created by the tensions between the two types of soldier portrayed in the patrol: the professionals, Mitchem and Johnstone, who volunteered, and the rest, particularly Bamforth, who, as conscripts, are really only civilians in uniform.

The difference between the two types is most obvious in the argument over the fate of the Japanese prisoner.

The first audience

It is important to understand the historical setting of the play in order to be able to appreciate how Willis Hall has made his drama gripping. The audience either knows or can guess at the fate of the patrol as the Japanese army closes in on the British land forces in and around Singapore. The petty squabbles and personal rivalries among the men, played out against the background of what was then recent history, made the drama all the more compelling for its original audience.

The memory of the devastating defeat at Singapore would have been relatively fresh in the minds of Willis Hall's audience watching the play when it was first produced at the Nottingham Playhouse in September 1958. Because of National Service, a form of compulsory military conscription, many would also be familiar with life in the armed services both during the war and after. The National Services (Armed Forces) Act, passed by the British parliament at the outbreak of war in September 1939, provided for the conscription of all able-bodied men between the ages of 18 and 41 who were not in reserved occupations (those, like farming and mining, regarded as essential to the war effort) for the duration of the conflict. Though very unpopular, National Service continued after the war. Men between the ages of 18 and 21 had to serve in the armed forces for two years. The system was abolished in 1960.

Some of Willis Hall's audience could well have been veterans of the Second World War as well as of Britain's colonial conflicts in Africa and the Far East. They would have been familiar with the army slang which had become part of the nation's vocabulary, and the types to be found in groups of men brought together in this way, each of whom had his own means of coping with the experience.

Familiar, too, would be the ill-preparedness, the poor equipment, the social attitudes and the cynicism of the men. This realistic portrayal of army life contrasts sharply with that to be found in plays written after the First World War and illustrates a change in the British people's attitudes towards war as a whole. It also illustrates postwar developments in British theatre where, in the work of writers such as John Osborne, Arnold Wesker and Shelagh Delaney, there was a move towards greater social realism.

Attitudes to war

Throughout history wars have inspired a variety of creative responses, often from the men and women who fought in them. Ironically, out of the terrible suffering of the twentieth century's global conflicts has come some of the greatest literature of our times. The First World War (1914–18) inspired on all sides of the conflict an unprecedented outpouring of literature, particularly of poetry. The nature of that response changed as the war progressed and the casualties mounted. What began in 1914 with the romanticism of poets such as Rupert Brook, ended with the revulsion evident in the poems of Wilfred Owen and Siegfried Sassoon. Their writing changed for ever the way in which poets and all serious writers could portray war.

The First World War led to a general anti-war feeling among the British in the years that followed. Yet they entered the Second World War with a weary acceptance of the need to fight, albeit with an awareness of the likely sacrifices that lay ahead. The tone of much Second World War poetry reveals this feeling and there is some evidence of it in *The Long and the Short and the Tall*.

This is not a straightforwardly anti-war play. However, Willis Hall's characters do sometimes express attitudes towards war. On one hand we have the opinions of the professional soldier as expressed by Mitchem who, having experienced the brutal reality of war, has no illusions about it. On the other we have the humane but naïve notions of Macleish who has never been in combat and imagines that war can be fought according to rules.

The long and the short and the tall

They say there's a troopship just leaving
   Bombay,
Bound for Old Blighty shore,
Heavily laden with time-expired men,
Bound for the land they adore.
There's many a soldier just finishing his
   time,
There's many a twirp signing on.
You'll get no promotion this side of the
   ocean,
So cheer up, my lads, bless 'em all!

Bless 'em all! Bless 'em all!
The long and the short and the tall;
Bless all the sergeants and WOs, *
Bless all the corp'rals and their blinkin'
   sons,
'Cos we're saying goodbye to them all,
As back to their billets they crawl,
You'll get no promotion this side of the
   ocean,
So cheer up, my lads, bless 'em all!

They say, if you work hard you'll get better
   pay,
We've heard it all before,
Clean up your buttons and polish your
   boots,
Scrub out the barrack-room floor.
There's many a rookie has taken it in,
Hook line and sinker an' all,
You'll get no promotion this side of the
   ocean,
So cheer up, my lads, bless 'em all!

Bless 'em all! *etc*

They say that the Sergeant's a very nice
   chap,
Oh! What a tale to tell!
Ask him for leave on a Saturday night
He'll pay your fare home as well.
There's many a soldier has blighted his
   life,
Thro' writing rude words on the wall,
You'll get no promotion this side of the
   ocean,
So cheer up, my lads, bless 'em all!

Bless 'em all! *etc*

They say that the Corp'ral will help you
   along,
Oh! What an awful crime,
Lend him your razor to clean up his chin,
He'll bring it back every time.
There's many a rookie has fell in the
   mud,
Thro' leaving his horse in the stall,
You'll get no promotion this side of the
   ocean,
So cheer up, my lads, bless 'em all!

Bless 'em all! *etc*

Nobody knows what a twirp you've been,
So cheer up, my lads, bless 'em all!

*Warrant Officers

There is cynicism in the attitudes of some of the characters and yet there is pragmatism too. Most pressing for the men is the situation in which they find themselves and how they might safely get out of it.

The significance of the title

The title of the play is taken from a popular song of the Second World War. The lyrics express the hostility of the conscripted men towards those who find themselves comfortable home postings while they have to do all the fighting. The word 'Bless' is entirely **ironic** (see Literary Terms) in its meaning here. When sung by the men of the British army it was replaced by an obscenity. The men of the patrol are a mixed bunch. They come from different regions of the United Kingdom; they have different personalities; their experience of war varies.

They are the ... *Long and the Short and the Tall* of the title.

The setting of the play

This is a single set play: all the action takes place in the interior of an abandoned miners' hut somewhere in the jungle north of Singapore. The tension in the play is in part heightened by the enforced intimacy of the men and by the heat of the jungle. In this context the character traits of the men, in particular Bamforth's resistance to authority, Johnstone's sadism and Whitaker's nervousness and ineptitude, are brought sharply into focus. The deliberation over the fate of the prisoner, who shares this small space with his captors, focuses the attention of the audience on the central issue of war: the killing of another human being.

This is a thought-provoking play. Willis Hall gives the audience no help in determining who is right and who is wrong. He simply presents us with the a situation that best illustrates the brutal reality of war.

Part two

Summaries

General summary

Act I Part 1
(pages 1–27)
A disparate
group of
individuals

A group of soldiers on patrol in the Malayan jungle in 1942 stops for a rest in a deserted miners' hut. They have lost contact with headquarters, their radio is not working properly. They are a 'mixed bunch' of personalities, five conscripted men led by two non-commissioned officers (NCOs, officers below the rank of First Lieutenant: Sergeant-Major, Sergeant, Corporal, Lance-Corporal) who are professional soldiers.

The conscripted men do not seem to be particularly good soldiers. As their behaviour and their conversation reveal, they are all to some extent cynical about the army and the war. The action in this first section of the play hinges on Bamforth and his relationships with the other men. He is a 'barrack-room lawyer', constantly testing the authority of others and, even in his quiet moments, subtly insubordinate.

His disregard for Corporal Johnstone's authority and his goading of the newly promoted Macleish create the tension in the early part of the play. Bamforth and Macleish almost come to blows while the two NCOs are outside the hut. Mitchem restores order as soon as he returns, demonstrating his capability as a leader.

Act I Part 2
(pages 28–50)
The capture of
a Japanese
soldier

The men are at first unaware of how close the Japanese are. Their weak radio then picks up the voice of a Japanese radio operator. The conscripted men react with stark fear. Mitchem shows leadership and restores their confidence. He gives the order to move out.

Before they can do so, Bamforth spots a Japanese soldier coming up the trail towards the hut. A panic-stricken Whitaker leaves the radio set where it is visible to the soldier when he enters the hut to investigate. Johnstone captures the soldier and orders the men in turn to kill the man. Only Bamforth is willing to do so but is prevented by Mitchem.

Mitchem decides they should take the prisoner back to headquarters for interrogation. Faced with the enemy for the first time, the conscripted men react differently. Whitaker is plainly terrified while Bamforth gradually comes to like the captive, seeing him as a fellow human being. Macleish and Smith, who have been sent to reconnoitre the area, return and reveal the true extent of the patrol's predicament: it is virtually surrounded. At the end of Act I the radio bursts into life as a Japanese operator threatens in broken English 'We you come to get.'

Act II
The fate of the
prisoner

The Japanese soldier is at first very much the enemy. But, as the play progresses, we learn that he has a wife and children, one of them a newborn baby. At one point it appears as if he has looted cigarettes and a cigarette case from a British soldier. The men seem willing to kill him for that until Bamforth reveals that Whitaker, the clumsily inept radio operator, collects Japanese military souvenirs. We also see that the position of the Japanese prisoner might mirror that of Macleish's younger brother who has been posted 'up country'.

As the seriousness of their situation increases, Mitchem decides to kill the prisoner. Macleish is the first of the conscripted men to realise this. He objects but cannot counter Mitchem's soldierly logic. When the time comes to move out Bamforth, too, realises what is planned for the prisoner. He calls on the others to make a stand with him against Johnstone and Mitchem. None of them is prepared to do so. A struggle occurs between Mitchem, Johnstone and

Bamforth. During this, Whitaker panics and shoots the prisoner dead.

The sound of the gunshots alert the Japanese to the presence of the men in the hut. A brief fight ensues off-stage during which all the men, except Johnstone, are killed. The wounded Johnstone crawls back into the hut, lights one of the Japanese soldier's cigarettes and prepares to surrender.

Detailed summaries

Act 1 part 1 (pages 1–27)

Arrival at the hut

The patrol consists of three NCOs (non-commissioned officers): Sergeant Mitchem, the patrol's leader, Corporal Johnstone, his second in command, Lance-Corporal Macleish, and four conscripted men. Mitchem and Johnstone are professional soldiers, the others are men conscripted into the army as a result of the war. As Lance-Corporal, Macleish holds the lowest non-commissioned rank which places him just above Bamforth, Smith, Evans and Whitaker in terms of military authority. The patrol's mission is to look for signs of the Japanese advance on Singapore.

The patrol have lost contact with their base, some fifteen miles away. The battery in their radio is faulty though Whitaker, the radio operator, continues his attempts to contact base. Mitchem seems in control of the situation right from the start of the play. He decides that they should rest for 'half an hour at the most' (p. 3) before moving off back to camp, much to the relief of the men. Johnstone has his first confrontation with Bamforth who has removed his pack and is resting stretched out on the floor. Bamforth's facetiousness is immediately apparent too. He makes no attempt to disguise his dislike of Johnstone. When Johnstone orders him to put his pack back on, he looks to Mitchem for confirmation of the order 'BAMFORTH *glances across at* MITCHEM' (p. 2). This early action establishes Bamforth as a 'barrack-room lawyer' in the eyes of the audience.

Notice how differently the men behave when the NCOs have left.

Mitchem and Johnstone go off to reconnoitre the area leaving Macleish in charge. With the two professional soldiers out of the way, the men can relax. Bamforth brags about what he will do to Johnstone when he gets him back to 'civvy street' where the latter's superior rank no longer counts. The others seem to have heard all this before. Bamforth is challenged first by Smith who complains of 'Bloody southerners shouting the odds. Always shouting the odds. You're like all the rest. One look at a barmaid and you're on the floor' (p. 6). Bamforth ignores this and continues his mockery of Evans. Note how Bamforth, using sarcasm and humour, is able to manipulate the situation as he likes. Having grossly insulted Evans in one breath he subtly ingratiates himself with the next, 'Very crafty boys, these Taffs. You've got to hand it to them' (p. 6), in order to obtain a cigarette.

Macleish becomes Bamforth's butt.

Macleish reacts angrily to Bamforth's criticism of Johnstone, a fellow NCO. At this point in the play

Macleish represents authority in Bamforth's eyes and for this reason warrants particular attention. First, he insults Macleish's nationality. When Macleish reacts by trying to assert his superior rank, Bamforth mocks him by sarcastically paraphrasing King's Regulations (now Queen's Regulations: the legally enforceable code of conduct which defines the relationships between the different ranks in the British army). Unable to match Bamforth for banter, Macleish dismisses him as 'a nutter' (p. 8). Bamforth responds by singing a song which glorifies his own abilities at fighting. Whitaker, who has been continuing to try to contact base, objects but Bamforth continues to sing to the irritation of the others. We learn here that the patrol is about fifteen miles from base. Whitaker is sure he has heard something on the radio. Bamforth is scornful; the others are anxious he continues to try to make contact.

Once again Macleish attempts to assert his authority over Bamforth and rein him in. Bamforth resists him, turning Macleish's insistence upon discipline against him 'Eight-double-seven Private Bamforth to you, Corporal Macleish. You want to come the regimental, boy, we'll have it proper' (p. 10). Macleish is supported in his attempts by Smith. With Evans as his foil, Bamforth uses humour to undermine Macleish and Smith. Then, having tired of the banter, he relaxes.

Bamforth turns his attention to Evans.

Bamforth begins to read the magazine, *Ladies' Companion and Home*, Evans has brought with him, then uses Evans's enjoyment of the serial as an opportunity for more humorous banter. The others join in. Bamforth turns to the 'Problems Answered' page, reading out a letter and inventing a reply which insults corporals. Evans naïvely believes it is a real reply.

It emerges in the conversation that follows that Evans has a girlfriend back home whom he has not seen for eighteen months. Bamforth again uses this as an opportunity for amusement at Evans's expense. We hear some details of Evans's home life and then of Smith's.

A fight breaks out. Bamforth returns to his attack on Evans (p. 16) pursuing the theme of his girlfriend's supposed imaginings. Evans reacts angrily this time and the two fight. He is no physical match for Bamforth who overpowers and humiliates him, letting him go only when Whitaker thinks he has got through on the radio set. Next Bamforth turns his attention to Whitaker, mocking him and saying he is trying to curry favour with Mitchem.

Angrily, Bamforth examines his rations, exclaiming 'Bloody cheese again' (p. 18). Evans wonders aloud why they are on patrol in the first place. Smith and Bamforth are equally cynical in their replies. As Whitaker darns his socks for kit inspection, Bamforth outlines his plans for escape (p. 19) should the enemy appear.

Macleish intervenes again, but Bamforth will not be silenced. His remarks are now intended specifically to irritate Macleish. He challenges Macleish who threatens him 'I'll have you' (p. 22). Bamforth further challenges him to take off his tape and repeat the threat. Macleish struggles to control himself and has to be restrained by Smith. All eyes are now on Bamforth and Macleish. Violence is about to break out when Mitchem and Johnstone re-enter the hut.

The NCOs return and discipline is restored. Order is immediately restored. Mitchem brings the patrol to attention and demands to know what has been happening. Macleish is unwilling to implicate Bamforth. It is only when Mitchem threatens to punish the whole patrol that Bamforth steps forward. Mitchem's long speech at this point includes a severe dressing-down for Bamforth. He also explains what he and Johnstone have discovered up the track. He then tells the patrol that they are to move off in fifteen minutes. We learn that Macleish's brother is with the British advance forces.

COMMENT

Note how Willis Hall quickly establishes the characters in the minds of his audience by what they say or do and how they interact with one another. That Johnstone and Bamforth do not like one another is apparent from the outset. They have their first confrontation on page 2 when Bamforth removes his pack and lies down without permission. Mitchem appears decisive here, issuing orders and intervening between Bamforth and Johnstone.

Note here too the use of language (see Commentary – Language & Style). Johnstone orders the men to hurry up using the Malay 'Gillo! Lacas!' (p. 2). Here and throughout the dialogue is peppered with English military slang 'It's dead. Still dis. U/s' (p. 3). The effect of this is to add to the realism of the action. The characters are convincing as soldiers and as a group of men communicating with each other. The relationships between the characters are established largely through the way they speak or react to each other. Compare, for example, the way Bamforth speaks to Johnstone with the way he reacts to Mitchem's instructions.

The playwright deliberately emphasises the less pleasant aspects of Bamforth's character.

It is Bamforth who dominates the early action. The reaction of the audience to him at this point must be mixed. He, like the others, is a recognisable type, a real 'barrack-room lawyer', always sticking up for his own rights while at the same time bullying and preying on those weaker than himself, notably Evans, Macleish and Whitaker. Yet he is also quick-witted and funny. Consider what are our initial impressions of Bamforth.

Whitaker is the youngest of the men in the patrol. Bamforth reserves some of his most cruel humour for him. Bamforth mockingly disparages him as 'ten-thumbed Whitaker' (p. 9). This serves to emphasise the least attractive aspect of Bamforth's personality.

Throughout the early exchanges, in the absence of the two senior NCOs, Macleish tries to assert himself over Bamforth who constantly quotes King's Regulations, insisting upon being referred to by his number, rank and name, as regulations require. However, Smith's scornful intervention 'That will be the day, Bamforth. When you can work it regimental' (p. 10) prevents a confrontation for the time being. Bamforth, typically, pursues the line of banter to a humorous conclusion and then lies down to relax. He is also able to ignore or deflect the objections of Smith, a comparatively older family man, and exploit the sensitivity of the newly appointed Lance-Corporal Macleish.

Lack of humour makes Macleish an easy target. Macleish takes his responsibilities very seriously. This and his lack of humour make him especially vulnerable to Bamforth's mockery. Compare Macleish's attitude towards authority with Bamforth's.

The uneasy 'pecking order' among males thrown together in this way is familiar to us today and would have been even more so when the play was first performed and memories of compulsory military service were fresh in people's minds. The concerns of the men are petty: there is no discussion of issues relating to the war, no sense of a great and noble enterprise. Indeed, were it not for the characters' uniforms and the presence on stage of military hardware, this might be a group of workmates rather than soldiers.

The men are different from one another. This is emphasised in the way Bamforth attacks the others. His vicious joking tends to focus on his victim's geographical origins. The Welshman Evans bears the brunt of Bamforth's scorn. 'What do you know about it, you ugly foreigner? Get back to Wales, you Cardiff creep. Only good for digging coal and singing hymns, your crummy lot' (p. 5). He attempts to silence Macleish with 'Ah, shut up, you Scotch haggis!' (p. 7). Bamforth is a Londoner whose arrogance is born of his sense of superiority over the others, all of whom are from the provinces.

It is through Bamforth that Willis Hall emphasises a pervading cynicism among the men towards war. This theme is developed as the play progresses. Oddly, we might think, there is no sense at this stage of the play being overtly 'anti war'. The men do not think deeply about their reasons for fighting. Bamforth's liking for violence is apparent in his dealings with Evans and Macleish, but so too is his instinct for self-preservation as shown by his plans for escape in the event of the enemy's advance. This is quite deliberate. It adds to the realism of the play. Willis Hall emphasises the unglamorous routine of war, a theme of the play (see Commentary – Themes) as a whole. This is a *routine* patrol, the battery in their radio is almost dead, the men are tired and bored. Far from being eager to fight, they are desperate to get back to base. There is little sense in these early exchanges between the men that they are comrades in arms. They are a group of ordinary men – the ... *Long and the Short and the Tall* of the title.

Consider what the confrontation between Bamforth and Macleish tells us about Bamforth and how this is significant in terms of events later in the play.

This section of the play ends with a long speech by Mitchem in which he puts Bamforth firmly in his place and re-establishes discipline.

GLOSSARY   **Gillo** move quickly

Lacas hurry up

stag sentry duty

dis out of order

U/s abbreviation for unserviceable or useless

compo composition pack containing a day's rations

haircut to breakfast time at all times

tapes stripes indicating rank

bints girls

bog latrine

doolally weak and ineffective; from the name of a British
military sanatorium at Deolali, Bombay, in India

Fred Karno's mob musical hall troupe whose act portrayed comic
incompetence

Looey lieutenant

judies girls

Blighty England (from the Hindustani word *bilayati*)

bull empty talk

snappers children

drum house

bungy rations

NAAFI canteens for the armed forces run by the Navy, Army and
Air Forces Institute

detail ordered to do a particular duty

PBI poor bloody infantry

Tojo Japanese Prime Minister, 1941–44

Rising Sun symbol on the Japanese flag

yellow peril the Japanese threat

ab-dabs hysterical fit

call out the time give orders

cap and belt off the practice of removing a soldier's cap and
belt before submitting him to military justice

tripes entrails

barrack-room lawyer a soldier who makes trouble by insisting on
his rights

tick complaint

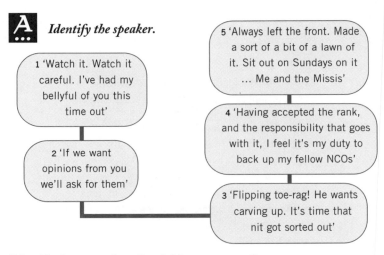

A *Identify the speaker.*

1 'Watch it. Watch it careful. I've had my bellyful of you this time out'

2 'If we want opinions from you we'll ask for them'

5 'Always left the front. Made a sort of a bit of a lawn of it. Sit out on Sundays on it ... Me and the Missis'

4 'Having accepted the rank, and the responsibility that goes with it, I feel it's my duty to back up my fellow NCOs'

3 'Flipping toe-rag! He wants carving up. It's time that nit got sorted out'

Identify the person 'to whom' this comment refers.

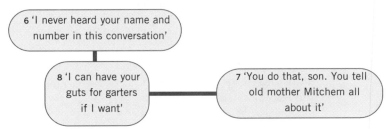

6 'I never heard your name and number in this conversation'

8 'I can have your guts for garters if I want'

7 'You do that, son. You tell old mother Mitchem all about it'

Check your answers on page 69.

B *Consider these issues.*

a Our impression of the characters up to the end of this section.

b Mitchem's leadership qualities.

c Bamforth's relationship with Johnstone.

d How the author conveys the attitudes of the men in the patrol towards the army and the war.

e How the author suggests Macleish's unease with his recent promotion.

f Consider how realistic this is as a portrayal of a group of soldiers at war.

ACT I PART 2 (PAGES 28–50)

Mitchem places Bamforth and Evans on guard, then encourages Whitaker to keep trying to contact base. Johnstone wonders what Whitaker picked up on the battery 'It could have been something important' (p. 29). Mitchem dismisses the possibility. They discuss what they are planning to do when they return to camp.

Consider the characters' different reactions when they hear a Japanese voice on the radio.

Suddenly, Whitaker does pick something up on the radio. The patrol's attention is focused on the set as it bursts into life – the voice of a Japanese radio operator is heard. The first reaction is uneasy humour. The atmosphere changes as they gradually realise the implications. Whitaker in particular is very afraid. Macleish wonders about his brother posted 'up country'. Mitchem then moves quickly to restore morale. He has the patrol load their guns then speaks to them to calm their nerves. He points out that they have heard one voice on the radio and that could mean only a handful of Japanese, a patrol like themselves. He expresses sympathy for whoever is in charge of the patrol. His humour defuses the tension.

The taking of the prisoner.

They are preparing to move out when Bamforth, who is still on guard at a window, spots movement outside. It is a Japanese soldier who is having a smoke. Bamforth makes as if to shoot him but is checked by Mitchem. The soldier finds the track and moves towards the hut. The patrol hide. In his panic, Whitaker leaves the radio set on the table where it is in full view of the door. There is no time to retrieve it as the soldier's footsteps can be heard on the verandah outside. The patrol wait for him to enter. As he does so, Johnstone lunges forward and grabs him. Mitchem goes outside to cover the jungle. Johnstone calls on Evans, Macleish and Smith in turn to kill the soldier with their bayonets. None of them is prepared to do so. Bamforth is about

to kill him when Mitchem re-enters and stops him.
Mitchem intends to take the prisoner back to camp
with them for interrogation and orders Bamforth to
disarm him.

The Japanese soldier is heavily armed and very
frightened. Johnstone expresses his disgust at the
unwillingness to kill on the part of Evans, Macleish and
Smith. Macleish counters with 'He was a prisoner of
war!' (p. 39). Johnstone points out that the prisoner was
heavily armed. Bamforth is ordered to guard the
prisoner. Bamforth torments the prisoner, issuing
orders in pidgin English. Johnstone expresses his
opinion that taking the prisoner with them is a risk.
Mitchem insists that they must. Macleish and Smith
are sent by Mitchem to reconnoitre further up the
track.

Mitchem tells the prisoner in broken English of their
plan to take him back to camp. Johnstone again
expresses his view that they should have killed him
immediately upon capture. He suggests killing him
before setting off. He wonders whether Mitchem is
'going soft' (p. 43). Mitchem at first points out that he
would have to write a report if they had killed the
prisoner. Johnstone dismisses this. Mitchem then

outlines his reasons for taking the prisoner back 'We've copped on to a lad who's going to make this detail worth its while' (p. 43). Mitchem makes it clear to Johnstone that he will kill the prisoner if it is necessary.

Slowly the transformation from stereotype enemy to human being begins.

To Johnstone's disgust, Mitchem allows the prisoner to take out his wallet which contains photographs of his family. We see the beginnings of a relationship forming between Bamforth and the prisoner 'He's almost human this one is!' (p. 45). Bamforth gives the prisoner a cigarette and Johnstone knocks it out of his mouth. Bamforth reacts angrily. When Johnstone goes to destroy the prisoner's photographs, Bamforth strikes Johnstone. Bamforth is placed under open arrest.

Macleish and Smith return with news of enemy troop movement further up the track. This development means the patrol must delay their march back to camp until dark. It also seals the fate of the prisoner. 'We're ditching him' (p. 49) is Mitchem's response to a question from Johnstone.

Urged by Mitchem to try to contact camp one more time, Whitaker again picks up the voice of a Japanese radio operator. This time his taunts can be heard very clearly. As the curtain falls on Act I the attention of the patrol, and that of the audience, focuses on the prisoner who, trying to please his captors, slowly puts his hands on his head.

COMMENT

The contrast in the leadership qualities of Mitchem and Johnstone is well established.

The return to the hut of the professional soldiers restores order for the time being. Notice the emergence of differences of opinions between Mitchem and Johnstone in this section of the play even before the capture of the Japanese prisoner. Consider whether Johnstone's views about what is the best course of action in a given situation can be considered as a serious alternative to Mitchem's. Note that Johnstone was right when he said that the indistinct voices picked up by Whitaker on the set were important (p. 29).

We see Mitchem at his best when the patrol are startled by the Japanese voice on the radio (p. 30). He skilfully restores their morale with humour and decisiveness. Could Johnstone have done this?

To kill, or not to kill, the prisoner?

The capture of the Japanese soldier is a defining moment in the play. It is an episode of high drama. What has in some ways been a domestic drama of character interaction suddenly focuses on the single issue of war: the killing of another human being. A major theme of the play is activated at this point. Johnstone and Bamforth (on two occasions) are prepared to kill the prisoner. The rest cannot bring themselves to use a bayonet. Finally, Mitchem decides to spare the man's life for sound military reasons.

The audience are confronted, in the immediate aftermath of the capture, with the conflicting views of Johnstone and Macleish. What are we to make of Macleish's argument that he was already a prisoner of war and therefore should not be killed? To what extent can we sympathise with Johnstone's view that, heavily armed as he was, the prisoner could have killed them all? (p. 39).

Bamforth resembles Johnstone in his willingness to kill the prisoner, probably indicating a sadistic streak in his nature, evidence of which we have seen earlier in the play. Yet in this section it is Bamforth who warms to the prisoner and slowly begins to see him as a man, particularly after looking at photographs of his family.

Like the men in the patrol, Willis Hall deliberately made the Japanese prisoner an ordinary man, so emphasising the difficulty of the decision whether, or not, to kill him.

We are not surprised by Johnstone's racism or by Bamforth's treatment of the prisoner. The behaviour and the language (see Commentary – Language & Style) of both characters serves to emphasise the realism of the play. Nevertheless, we can see in their attitudes, particularly in the change in Bamforth's, the development of another theme – that of human dignity (see Commentary – Themes).

Mitchem's pragmatism is in contrast to Johnstone's reflexive sadism. His reasoning behind keeping the prisoner alive makes military sense. Nevertheless, how far can we agree with Johnstone's counter argument that taking him back with them will make a difficult journey even more so? In finally deciding that the prisoner must die so that the patrol survives, Mitchem proves capable of making the most difficult of decisions when circumstances demand.

By the end of Act I, with the discovery that the Japanese are aware of the patrol's presence, the rights and wrongs of killing the prisoner become the audience's sole concern.

GLOSSARY

SOB son of a bitch

duff useless

roll on exasperated longing for the end of the war (duration)

geisha girls Japanese hostesses trained to entertain men with singing and dancing

crumb contemptible person or thing

gripe complain

joskins raw recruits

ginks men

Harry disparaging term, from music hall comedian Harry Tate

press, up to up to the present moment

swallow a short smoke
nub cigarette end
hump annoy; load
Rita Hayworth glamorous film star of the time
Geneva Convention international agreement governing the
 treatment of prisoners of war first formulated in 1864
mockers, put the mockers on prevent
muckers pals (men who muck in together)
dinky-doo rhyme for two
kybosh, put the kybosh on prevent, stop

A Identify the speaker.

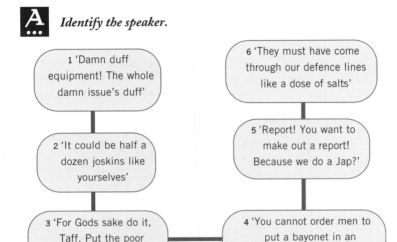

1 'Damn duff equipment! The whole damn issue's duff'

6 'They must have come through our defence lines like a dose of salts'

2 'It could be half a dozen joskins like yourselves'

5 'Report! You want to make out a report! Because we do a Jap?'

3 'For Gods sake do it, Taff. Put the poor bastard out of his misery'

4 'You cannot order men to put a bayonet in an unarmed prisoner'

Identify the person 'to whom' this comment refers.

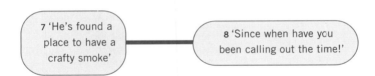

7 'He's found a place to have a crafty smoke'

8 'Since when have you been calling out the time!'

Check your answers on page 69.

B Consider these issues.

a The reasons why Mitchem decides to spare the prisoner's life.

b Why Evans, Macleish and Smith are unable to kill the prisoner.

c What Johnstone's motives are for wanting to kill the prisoner.

d Why Bamforth becomes friendly with the prisoner.

e How the author encourages our sympathy for the prisoner.

f How the author produces dramatic tension as the Act comes to a close.

ACT II   Thirty minutes have elapsed since the end of Act I.
                Macleish is guarding the prisoner, Bamforth, Evans and
                Johnstone are asleep and Smith and Whitaker stand
                guard at windows. The conversation between these two
                characters reveals that Whitaker likes to buy and sell
                items of jewellery in the NAAFI back at base.

                Mitchem tells Macleish to give the prisoner a drink of
                water. As he does so, Macleish observes that the
                prisoner doesn't seem to be a 'bad sort of bloke' (p. 53).
                Macleish is thinking of his brother and wonders
                whether he might have been captured too. He seems to
                be seeking reassurance from Mitchem that the stories
                he has heard about the enemy's treatment of prisoners
                are untrue. Mitchem, however, will not be drawn on
                the point.

Note Mitchem's   Macleish pursues the point 'He's human at least'
cynicism about   (p. 55). Mitchem draws on his experience of the effect
war and how it   a uniform can have on a man. He knows that men
contrasts with   behave differently when they join up and are posted
Macleish's   abroad. He has seen it many times before. Macleish
attitude.   seems not to understand. He voices his doubt about
                      whether he could kill if called upon to do so. Mitchem
                      assures him that he will and advises Macleish not to
                      think too much.

A long speech from Mitchem follows in which he outlines his personal philosophy about why men join the army. He blames women, 'bints' (p. 56), claiming that men join up hoping to impress a woman with the uniform.

Mitchem advises Macleish to 'drop the home and bint and family bull' (p. 57) or he might end up in the same position as the prisoner. From this point the truth slowly dawns on Macleish. When he finally realises what Mitchem has in mind for the prisoner he is appalled 'He's a POW!' (p. 58). He is further horrified by the method of dispatch – the bayonet. Mitchem points out that his priority is to get the patrol safely back to base and all other considerations are secondary. Mitchem dismisses the alternative solutions suggested by Macleish. But Macleish is not persuaded by Mitchem's dispassionate logic: 'It's bloody murder, man!' (p. 60). Mitchem simply states that murder is his job. Macleish has no answer to this.

Macleish accepts a cigarette from the prisoner. Mitchem rouses the sleeping Johnstone, Bamforth and Evans. Bamforth goes outside.

Mitchem tells Johnstone of his decision concerning the prisoner. Johnstone offers to kill him. Mitchem is irritated by Johnstone's harping on the subject.

Johnstone's racism is again evident. Johnstone notices that the prisoner is smoking a cigarette. He asks who gave him permission. Macleish explains that it is one of the prisoner's own. Johnstone then realises it is a British cigarette. The atmosphere changes as the men, including Macleish and Evans, realise the implications – that the prisoner has looted the cigarettes from a British prisoner. Goaded by Johnstone, they advance threateningly on the prisoner. Mitchem stops them and orders Macleish to search the prisoner for more stolen items. Johnstone takes the prisoner's wallet and slowly tears his photographs into pieces.

At this point, Bamforth re-enters. He announces that it was he who gave the prisoner the cigarettes. Macleish and Evans are shamefaced. Evans attempts to atone by picking up the pieces of the prisoner's photographs and suggesting they might be stuck back together. Johnstone demands to see the prisoner's cigarette case. When it transpires that the case is British made, the atmosphere of hostility returns.

Bamforth's defence of the prisoner is forceful and effective.

Bamforth interposes himself between the prisoner and the others. He scoffs at their reasoning, pointing out that his own sister has a Japanese-made doll. He further points out that Whitaker collects Japanese souvenirs. Despite Smith's attempts to protect him, Whitaker is forced to admit this. He goes on to explain that he acquired the souvenirs by swopping them at the UJ Club at base. As a result Bamforth successfully persuades the others that the prisoner might have acquired the cigarette case quite innocently.

The atmosphere is calm again. Evans even accepts a cigarette from the prisoner. In this interlude, as Smith encourages him to talk, we learn of Whitaker's girlfriend in Darlington. He has not received a letter from her for six weeks and has given up hope of hearing from her again. Bamforth sings 'quietly and with a touch of sadness' (p. 80).

This time Bamforth's defence of the prisoner fails.

The patrol prepares to move off and Bamforth offers the prisoner a drink of water. Johnstone stops him. In the following exchange Bamforth realises that the prisoner is to be killed. He objects 'What's the poor get done to us?' (p. 82). He once again puts himself between the prisoner and the rest of the patrol, defying Mitchem's instruction to move out of the way. He calls on Whitaker, Evans, Smith and Macleish in turn to side with him. Whitaker is too afraid, Evans and Smith seem to go along with Mitchem's logic.

Whitaker is ordered to cover the prisoner with the sten as Mitchem and Johnstone move to overpower Bamforth. The prisoner, who has realised the implications, rises and is shot dead by a panic-stricken Whitaker. Bamforth sarcastically comments that Whitaker has another souvenir. Mitchem's patience finally snaps and he hits Bamforth.

Realising that the shots will have alerted the Japanese, Mitchem orders the men to move out. He knows they have no chance of making it back so tells Johnstone to make one more attempt to contact base to inform them of the Japanese advance. There is no reply and Johnstone gives up. The men then leave the hut. They are immediately attacked. We hear the cries of dying men and the wounded Whitaker calling for his mother before being shot. Johnstone, also wounded, re-enters the hut. He hears the operator on the radio, picks up the hand-set and tells him to 'Get knotted!' (p. 86). He helps himself to one of the prisoner's cigarettes, ties the prisoner's white silk scarf to the barrel of his sten-gun and prepares to surrender.

COMMENT

Mitchem's experience helps him make difficult decisions.

The moral issues of the play are spelt out very clearly in the final act as the action moves towards its violent climax. At the opening of Act II the mood is subdued as the men await darkness before moving out. Macleish is worried about his younger brother who has been posted to an advanced position He seeks reassurance from Mitchem who does not give him any. Macleish voices what might be the feelings of the audience towards the prisoner at this point, that he is above all a fellow human being. Mitchem knows from experience, however, that it is unwise to harbour such thoughts 'You get a bloke between your sights and stop to wonder if he's got a family, Jock, your family's not got you' (p. 55). Macleish nevertheless honestly doubts his ability to kill.

In the conversation that follows (p. 56), we gain some insight into Mitchem's personality. Consider how his assertion that 'Half the scrapping in this world is over judies' (p. 56) affects our sympathies towards him. Note how his cynicism seems to make him a more effective soldier in that he is able to make difficult decisions and to act upon them. Contrast this with Macleish's moral squeamishness.

Macleish represents the civilian viewpoint.

As far as Mitchem is concerned, the logic of their situation has dictated the fate of the prisoner, though Macleish is as yet unaware of this. This betrays Macleish's naïvety. The author is challenging his audience to consider the alternatives to Mitchem's decision to kill the prisoner. Whereas we might sympathise with Macleish's sense of moral outrage at the thought of what is in effect cold-blooded murder, the power of Mitchem's simple argument is compelling. Macleish has no answer to it. To what extent do his revulsion and his inability to refute the argument reflect the feelings of the audience?

In the end Macleish is reduced to silence. These exchanges between Mitchem and Macleish are crucial in understanding the author's own attitude towards the issue of killing the prisoner. Willis Hall had been a professional soldier. Mitchem's uncomplicated reasoning is that of the professional soldier doing his job regardless of the moral implications. Unlike Macleish, he is under no misapprehension about the true nature of war. When Macleish says 'It's bloody murder man!' (p. 60), he candidly admits 'Course it is. That is my job.' Mitchem sees no alternative to this. His rhetorical question '... what am I supposed to do? Turn conshi? Jack it in? Leave the world to his lot?' (p. 60) is the only allusion to a 'cause' worth fighting for.

Mitchem's scathing dismissal of what he believes to be Macleish's 'comic book' image of war is worthy of Bamforth in its sarcasm. It leaves Macleish utterly defeated.

Consider how our attitude towards Macleish is affected by his reaction towards the prisoner over his suspected looting of the British cigarette case. Note in contrast Mitchem's consistently dispassionate response.

Bamforth defends an enemy by attacking his own colleagues.

Bamforth's successful defence of the prisoner works by undermining the assumptions of the others, pointing out obvious facts, that goods are imported from abroad, for instance, but is most devastating when he succeeds in muddying the moral waters. He points out with withering sarcasm that the most cowardly and ineffectual member of the patrol, Whitaker 'The Tyneside hero' (p. 75), himself collects Japanese souvenirs, undoubtedly originally looted from the enemy but innocently obtained by him at the UJ Club. All but Johnstone are convinced, or at least silenced, by this argument.

We learn more about Whitaker's background in his conversation with Smith and this adds to our perception of him as young and pathetically inexperienced. It also increases the impact of the play's brutal **denouement** (see Literary Terms).

In the lull before what proves to be the final action, Bamforth sings a mournful song. Note how effectively this adds to the mood at this point.

Ironically, Bamforth's defence leads to the prisoner's death.

It is Bamforth's attempt to prevent the killing of the prisoner that brings the moral issue of the play most sharply into focus. Against Mitchem's 'It's something in a uniform and it's a different shade to mine' (p. 82), Bamforth almost desperately asserts 'He's a man!' When Bamforth calls him a 'bastard', Mitchem poignantly responds with 'I wish to God I was' (p. 82).

The failure of the others in the patrol to join Bamforth in his moral stand confirms our opinions of each of them. Whitaker, perfectly in character, opts for self-preservation. Evans, consistently dim-witted to the end, cites the cigarette case as reason enough to kill the man. Smith's 'I just take orders' (p. 83) is eerily redolent of the failed defence offered by Nazi war criminals at the Nuremburg trials after the Second World War. The **irony** (see Literary Terms) here is not lost on the audience. Macleish, guiltily aware of his powerlessness, says and does nothing. Again, Willis Hall seems to be inviting (daring?) his audience to choose. It is a moment of high drama.

The accidental shooting of the prisoner underlines our sense that this is a 'crumb patrol', as does Johnstone's survival and willingness to surrender. The wounded Whitaker's terrified cry 'Mother!' is followed by a single gunshot leaving us to assume, again **ironically**, that he has been executed. Consider, too, the **irony** in the closing moments of the play as 'Red Leader' finally responds on the radio set and Johnstone helps himself to one of the prisoner's cigarettes before signalling his surrender.

GLOSSARY

RSM Regimental Sergeant Major

gob drink

mugs away a phrase used in the game of darts meaning the losers of the last game (mugs) start the next

dancers stairs

conshi conscientious objector to fighting

shufti a look (from the Arabic word *saffa*)

snout cigarette

slot stab

gelt money (from the German word *geld*)

fives fists

UJ Club Union Jack Club for servicemen

butcher's look (rhyming slang, butcher's hook)

Bramah beautiful

buckshee free, without charge (from the Persian word *backsheesh*)

Identify the speaker.

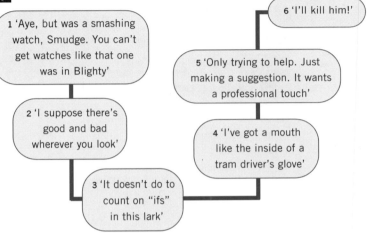

6 'I'll kill him!'

1 'Aye, but was a smashing watch, Smudge. You can't get watches like that one was in Blighty'

5 'Only trying to help. Just making a suggestion. It wants a professional touch'

2 'I suppose there's good and bad wherever you look'

4 'I've got a mouth like the inside of a tram driver's glove'

3 'It doesn't do to count on "ifs" in this lark'

Identify the person 'to whom' this comment refers.

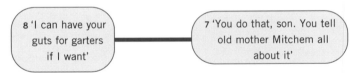

8 'I can have your guts for garters if I want'

7 'You do that, son. You tell old mother Mitchem all about it'

Check your answers on page 69.

B *Consider these issues.*

a The change in our attitude towards Mitchem in this Act.

b How Bamforth's relationship with the prisoner changes and what makes him risk his own life to protect him.

c How Mitchem is able to defeat Macleish's arguments about the fate of the prisoner.

d The differences between Johnstone and Mitchem in their attitude to the prisoner.

e The assumptions the audience and characters share about the prisoner.

PART THREE

COMMENTARY

THEMES

Willis Hall explores a number of themes in the play. They are issues that concern any ordinary person who finds himself or herself in the extraordinary circumstance of war. They are:

- the morality of killing
- attitudes towards war
- human dignity

The themes are interrelated and are explored through the thoughts, feelings and behaviour of the men in the patrol. However, the single most important event in the play, the capture of the Japanese soldier, acts as a catalyst that leads to the play's dramatic conclusion.

THE MORALITY OF KILLING

The Long and the Short and the Tall belongs to a **genre** (see Literary Terms) of postwar British theatre that is distinguished by its realistic portrayal of social and domestic issues. The attitudes of the characters in the play realistically represent a range of views towards killing:

- Johnstone is quite prepared to kill the prisoner immediately upon capture or later in cold blood. He is motivated by hatred.
- Mitchem arrives at the decision to kill by cold military logic. He neither relishes nor shrinks from the prospect.
- Macleish, whose instinctive humanity is compromised by the predicament in which he finds himself, feels revulsion at the thought of killing the prisoner.

- Bamforth is prepared to kill the prisoner at first but changes his mind once he comes to see him as an individual.

It is through Bamforth that Willis Hall voices the arguments of **moral relativism** (see Literary Terms). The central moral issue in the play is not clear-cut. We can share in Macleish's revulsion at the thought of killing, yet we must acknowledge the logic of Mitchem's argument. There is no simple right or wrong. This is the point Willis Hall makes about killing in war.

Mitchem does not disagree with Macleish when he says that killing the prisoner is murder. The difference between the two is that, unlike Macleish, Mitchem is aware that murder is his job.

He believes that 'It stinks' to kill the prisoner because war itself 'stinks' and that people like Macleish are fools for not realising that in the first place. He ridicules what he believes are Macleish's illusions about war fought according to the rules of a civilised society, as it is portrayed in comic books. For Mitchem, war has its own rules, quite different from those of society.

Whose side is the author on?

The choices faced by the men in the patrol are difficult. Willis Hall skilfully makes his audience share in the men's discomfiture by having Mitchem, a character with whom we can sympathise, argue persuasively in favour of killing the prisoner. We also see the irony in Bamforth's defence of the prisoner on the grounds that he is a fellow human being.

Smith, who by his own admission 'just plods on', represents another attitude, one held by those who would prefer not to do the deed themselves but are prepared to look the other way while others do it. When called on by Bamforth to stand with him in defence of the prisoner, he says 'I just do as I'm told', echoing the defence offered by German soldiers complicit in Second World War atrocities.

ATTITUDES TOWARDS WAR

The attitudes we hear expressed in the play towards war and the job of soldiering are at one with the realism of the drama as a whole. The men are all cynical about the army to some extent and this cynicism extends to the war itself. This can be seen most clearly in Bamforth's attitudes. Early in Act I Bamforth announces his intention of running away should the enemy arrive. We see it too in his **ironic** (see Literary Terms) reference to 'cartloads of glorious allies' (p. 14) and when he sarcastically remarks 'It's what we're fighting for. Loose living and six months' holiday a year' (p. 21).

Mitchem is a professional. He sees soldiering as a job. He has experienced war and has no illusions about how it must be fought. This enables him to decide what has to be done regardless of his personal feelings. Mitchem does not despise the enemy as Johnstone does. He sees the parallels between the Japanese and themselves. We see evidence of this in his speech in Act I after Whitaker first picks up the voice of the Japanese radio operator. Despite his belief that war as a whole 'stinks' he believes he has no choice but to fight. There is evidence of this in Act II when he explains to Macleish his reasons for deciding the prisoner must die. He scathingly debunks the popular misconceptions of war before saying what it is really like. For Mitchem, war is simply a matter of kill or be killed.

Johnstone is a wholly unsympathetic character who, like Mitchem, has no illusions about war. In the closing moments of the play, after the Japanese ambush,

Johnstone reveals his instinct for self-preservation, preferring to surrender rather than die fighting.

HUMAN DIGNITY

This theme is explored through the men's treatment of the Japanese prisoner. In 1958, when the play was first performed, feelings towards the Japanese were strongly influenced by memories of the atrocities they had committed and their treatment of British prisoners of war. In order to establish the prisoner's humanity in the minds of the audience, Willis Hall shows us how he resembles the men in the patrol in some important respects:

- his fate possibly mirrors that of Macleish's brother, posted up country where the Japanese have broken through.
- we see when he is first captured that he is as afraid of them as they are of him.
- though the prisoner may have looted the cigarette case, one of the patrol, Whitaker, also possesses looted property.
- like Smith, he has a wife and children.

The prisoner also mirrors the naïvety of the conscripted men in the patrol. Far from being a superhuman fighting machine we can speculate that perhaps it was the prisoner's inexperience that led to his capture. Both the audience and the characters come to see the prisoner as an individual and begin to experience feelings of unease about his fate. Bamforth quickly realises that the prisoner is indeed a man. It is this instinctive recognition of common humanity that leads him to share cigarettes with the prisoner and to insist that he has water.

Macleish voices the squeamishness of the audience over the fate of the prisoner. He confesses to Mitchem in

Act II his inability to kill at close quarters. It would be different were it at a distance 'Something moving about in the trees – something you can put a bullet in and not have to … have to look into its eyes' (p. 55).

For him it is the means of dispatch that appals as much as the fact that he is to die. Mitchem *can* bring himself to kill, but only by denying the humanity of the enemy, as he explains to Bamforth towards the end of Act II: 'It's something in a uniform and it's a different shade to mine' (p. 82).

The most extreme (and consistent) attitude is shown by Johnstone who treats the prisoner with utter contempt. From the moment of capture he is ready and willing to kill the prisoner, denying absolutely his human dignity.

STRUCTURE

The play is divided into two acts, the first much longer than the second. Within the two acts there are several clear shifts in the action.

ACT I

The first part of Act I, up to the point where Bamforth and Macleish are about to fight when Mitchem and Johnstone re-enter the hut, can be considered separately from the remainder of the act. In this first section Willis Hall introduces the characters, giving details about their backgrounds and establishing relationships between them. In particular we see Bamforth as the typical bully as he first intimidates Evans and Whitaker then challenges Macleish's authority.

The men's cynicism (see Themes) about the war is explored here too. In the absence of Mitchem and Johnstone, who have left the hut to reconnoitre the surrounding jungle, Bamforth can give full rein to his sarcasm. Through him we hear the values and attitudes of the conscripted soldier. We see that they have no sense of why they are fighting. Their concerns are more to do with their personal lives. We gain a sense of their ordinariness. The details about their backgrounds help to do this.

Bamforth's humour establishes the tone at this point. On two occasions the pace of the action changes as violence threatens to erupt, once when Bamforth goads Evans, and again when his argument with Macleish almost blows up into a fight.

Although absent for the greater part of this section of Act I, we can contrast the brisk efficiency of Mitchem and Johnstone with the relaxed, sometimes slovenly, approach of the conscripted men.

The key event in the second half of Act I is the capture of the Japanese soldier and the beginning of the debate about his fate. Mitchem is master of the situation at this point. He orders that the prisoner's life be spared. In the reactions of the various members of the patrol we see confirmation of their personalities. Bamforth's initial willingness to kill is not surprising. His taking of the prisoner under his wing is. Again, there is a change in the pace of the action as violence erupts involving Bamforth, this time a fight with Johnstone.

The voice of the Japanese radio operator at the end of Act I is a moment of tension and high drama as it seals the prisoner's fate and leaves the audience wondering how the patrol will react to the changed circumstances.

ACT II   There is a lull in the action at the beginning of Act II as we hear of Whitaker's souvenir collecting, an effective change of pace after the tense note on which Act I ends. There follows a long conversation between Mitchem and Macleish in which both men make clear their views on the subject of killing. The conversation builds up to the moment when Macleish realises that

Mitchem has changed his mind about taking the prisoner back to base and instead is going to kill him.

The audience is challenged by the brutal simplicity of Mitchem's military logic. We are further challenged by the incident involving the cigarette case. Consider the impact of this on the audience. It affects our view of the Japanese soldier. We come to see that he and the men in the patrol are no different.

As the act builds towards its bloody **climax** (see Literary Terms) we learn of Whitaker's girlfriend in Darlington. This emphasises his inexperience and his youth which in turn serves to increase the impact of the **denouement** (see Literary Terms).

CHARACTERS

SERGEANT MITCHEM

Mitchem is the leader of the patrol and an experienced professional soldier. He has the respect of the men who trust him to do the right thing. His orders are clear and direct. Until the very end of the play he seems to be in command of the situation.

It is Mitchem's experience that sets him apart from the conscripted men. Unlike Macleish, Mitchem has no illusions about war. He does not regard it as heroic and despises Macleish for not realising that. For Mitchem, soldiering is a job and he is concerned to do it well. In the play, his immediate job is to get the patrol safely back to base. Mitchem's decision to kill the prisoner is made in the light of this simple fact.

Strong leader
Pragmatist
Humane
Uncomplicated
Professional

Mitchem differs from Johnstone, his fellow NCO, in one important respect. Whereas Johnstone seems to be motivated by hatred of the enemy and an apparent love of violence, Mitchem takes no pleasure in killing. He arrives at his decision to kill the prisoner purely on the basis of practicality, emotion has no part in it. The logic of his argument finally undermines Macleish's objections. At the end of the play the rest of the patrol side with Mitchem rather than Bamforth who is prepared to defend the prisoner with his life.

Mitchem's
relations with
the men under
him.

Mitchem's relationship with Johnstone is an interesting one. They are, for the reasons outlined above, quite different – both as men and as soldiers. Throughout the play there is a **tension** (see Literary Terms) between the two that arises from differences in their approach to leadership. The tension is particularly evident in their attitudes towards the prisoner.

Johnstone had wanted to kill the heavily armed prisoner immediately upon capture, whereas Mitchem realised it would be more useful to take him back to base for interrogation. This proves to be a fateful decision since it is the accidental shooting of the prisoner at the end of the play that leads to the death of the men in the patrol. We could speculate upon what might have happened had Bamforth not been prevented from following Johnstone's order to kill him.

Despite this, Mitchem has undoubted leadership qualities that Johnstone does not possess. He does not depend upon verbal bullying and the threat of violence to sustain his authority as Johnstone does. He is skilful in his handling of both Whitaker and, until the very end of the play, Bamforth. Mitchem has seen Bamforth's type before and knows how to deal with him, this experience enabling him to defuse Bamforth's sarcasm. Bamforth for his part seems to realise that Mitchem has no obvious weaknesses to be exploited and therefore grudgingly accepts his authority.

Mitchem has a fatherly attitude towards Whitaker, calling him 'son' and encouraging him in his attempts to contact base, Mitchem's decisiveness steadies the men's nerves at crucial points in the action. For example, when Whitaker picks up the voice of a Japanese operator on the radio (p. 32), he moves quickly to restore their confidence by the clever use of humour and logic.

Mitchem's attitude to his job.

Bamforth calls Mitchem 'a dirty bastard' (p. 82) when he realises the prisoner will be killed, but is this judgement really fair? Mitchem expresses the view of the professional soldier. He is in command of the patrol and has clear priorities that in his view outweigh humanitarian concerns. Whereas Macleish is appalled by the thought of killing the prisoner in cold blood, Mitchem's reasoning leads him to only one conclusion: 'I've got six men and one report to come out of this … You reckon I should lose my sleep over him?' (p. 59). Mitchem is essentially a decent man, with whose dilemma the audience can have a great deal of sympathy. He also happens to be a soldier and, as such, accepts that it is necessary to kill. It is his decency which makes his logic so difficult to refute.

Mitchem has no grand theories about war and the job of being a soldier. He believes that many men join the army simply to impress women. From this we might guess at Mitchem's own reasons for joining. Nevertheless, in his conversation with Macleish in Act II, Mitchem reveals something of his motivation as a soldier. Because he has experienced combat, Mitchem has already rehearsed the arguments and reached a resolution of sorts over the dilemma which is exercising the mind of the inexperienced Macleish. Mitchem, a professional soldier and a character with whom the audience can have sympathy, articulates the abiding paradox of war. Killing the prisoner 'stinks' he says, but 'the whole lot stinks to me. So what am I supposed to do? Turn conshi? Jack it in? Leave the world to his lot?'

(p. 60). While there is in his remarks an unequivocal acknowledgement of the prisoner's humanity there is an equally unquestioning acceptance of the necessity to fight and to kill – because he believes there is no alternative. In Mitchem the audience sees how a soldier, an otherwise decent man, can arrive psychologically at a position where he is able to do his job and all that it entails: 'It's a war. It's something in a uniform and it's a different shade to mine' (p. 82).

CORPORAL JOHNSTONE

Johnstone is second in command of the patrol and, like Mitchem, a professional soldier. He is foul mouthed, bigoted and sadistic, perhaps the only character with whom the audience can have no sympathy whatsoever. He provides a stark contrast with Mitchem's style of leadership. Whereas Mitchem is capable of persuading the men, Johnstone harangues and bullies them. We see this most forcefully in his dealings with Bamforth with whom he is constantly on the brink of conflict. Nevertheless, we might reason that had Johnstone succeeded in killing the prisoner immediately upon capture the patrol might have survived.

Sadistic
Bully
Bigoted
Survivor

Despite this, Johnstone does not represent an alternative leadership option for the patrol because we sense that the men would not follow him. Rather Johnstone's character serves to throw Mitchem's into greater relief. He shares Mitchem's soldierly logic but does not have his obvious qualms about killing since he lacks Mitchem's humanity and his judgement is clouded by hatred of the enemy. Mitchem's initial decision to take the prisoner back to base for interrogation is based on sound military reasoning. Johnstone's willingness to kill him, however, is motivated by apparent racism and a love of violence. When the decision is made to kill the prisoner, Johnstone volunteers to do the job (p. 65). There is a clear note of disgust in Mitchem's response 'Do you know, I think you would at that.' When it is suspected that the prisoner has looted British cigarettes, Johnstone '*slowly and carefully, tears the [prisoner's] photographs into pieces*' (p. 68). It is Johnstone who constantly stirs the antagonism of the men towards the prisoner. To Johnstone, the prisoner is not a human being.

Though wounded, Johnstone alone survives the Japanese attack at the end of the play, ironically helping himself to one of the dead prisoner's cigarettes while preparing to surrender. It is **ironic** (see Literary Terms), too, that Johnstone, so eager to kill throughout the play, opts to surrender rather than to die fighting.

BAMFORTH

Bamforth is completely cynical about the war and the army (see Themes). Our initial impression of him is as a barrack-room lawyer, someone who has learned the rules of the army and uses them to his own advantage. He constantly tests the authority of those in command, particularly Johnstone with whom he is always at odds. Bamforth has the intelligence and wit to frustrate Johnstone's attempts to keep him in his place.

Bamforth also uses his cruel wit to ridicule the weaker personalities in the patrol, Evans and Whitaker, neither of whom has the intelligence, humour or physical strength to defend himself adequately against Bamforth's bullying. He is in many ways a character with whom the audience can have few sympathies. He seems arrogant and amoral at first, utterly lacking any soldierly qualities beyond a readiness to kill, responding to Johnstone's orders with reluctance, and cheekily outlining to the others his plans for escape in the event

Barrack-room lawyer
Insubordinate
Insolent
Reckless

of a Japanese attack: alone and disguised as a native. Yet he remains an attractive character. This is in part due to his humour, deployed effectively in his dealings with all others in the patrol except Mitchem, and his **ironic** (see Literary Terms) debunking of military pomposity. His is the voice of the reluctant soldier.

When the prisoner is first captured, only Bamforth is prepared to kill him with a bayonet, showing his lack of squeamishness when it comes to violence. It seems ironic that later he should be alone in objecting to the killing of the prisoner. Bamforth at first delights in tormenting his captive but warms to him once he discovers he has a family.

From this point on we see the humane side of Bamforth, quite at odds with our initial impression of him. In his defence of the prisoner against the assaults of the rest of the patrol Bamforth is acknowledging a fellowship with him (see Themes). His arguments are judicious and demonstrate a clarity of thought lacking in the others. Through him the writer expresses the moral uncertainty implicit in the willingness to kill. The prisoner might well be in possession of looted British cigarettes, but then Whitaker possesses looted Japanese property. By the end of the play Bamforth does not distinguish between the prisoner and the men in the patrol.

Yet his humanitarianism is instinctive and emerges only when he comes to recognise the prisoner as a man with a wife and family. Because Bamforth is not a soldier he does not understand the reasoning behind Mitchem's decision to kill the prisoner. This reveals Bamforth's naïvety, at least in military terms, and in this sense he is no different from his fellow conscripts. When he finally realises what Mitchem is planning to do he seems genuinely shocked. However, unlike his fellow conscripts, he is prepared to defend the prisoner's life with his own, recklessly disregarding the safety of his comrades. Paradoxically, Bamforth the bully who delighted in tormenting his weaker comrades earlier in the play, ends it as the voice of humanity. Against Mitchem's cold logic Bamforth can only cry 'He's a man!' (p. 82).

MACLEISH

Ill-equipped for authority
Decent
Idealistic
Naïve

Macleish is a newly promoted Lance-Corporal as yet uncertain of his position in the patrol. As a conscripted man he does not have the military nous of either Mitchem or Johnstone and is really only a civilian in uniform who has yet to experience real combat. Though he tries hard to perform his duties as an NCO when left in command of the patrol, he betrays weaknesses which Bamforth readily exploits. He is unwilling to kill the prisoner when the latter is first captured and is squeamish about doing so later in the play. Macleish expresses the horror most of the audience will feel at the prospect of killing a defenceless human being in cold blood. In his conversation with Mitchem in Act II he articulates what might be our own reticence about killing a man at close quarters with a bayonet, as distinct from at a distance with a rifle 'If it was him or me. Something moving about in the trees – something you can put a bullet in and not have to … have to look into its eyes' (p. 55).

Again, unlike Johnstone and Mitchem, he believes war can be fought according to rules. To this extent he is an idealist. Macleish's reticence about killing stems from his innate humanity and a recognition of the similarity between the plight of the prisoner and that of his younger brother who he believes may have been captured by the Japanese.

But his position on the issue is undermined first by Mitchem's cold logic and secondly by his own vacillating behaviour towards the prisoner: initially unwilling to kill the man himself, expressing disgust at Mitchem's decision to do so, joining in with the attack on the prisoner over the cigarettes, and finally acquiescing to Mitchem's decision. As a character, Macleish best embodies the moral confusion of war and the individual's unwillingness to confront it fully. Finally, when Bamforth calls on his support in defence of the prisoner, he *'continues to stare out of the window'* (p. 83).

THE JAPANESE SOLDIER

The Japanese soldier is described in the stage directions as *'a small, round, pathetic and almost comic character, armed to the teeth in Gilbertian fashion'* (p. 38). He is also afraid. For much of the Second World War the Japanese army was widely perceived by the Allies to be invincible and its soldiers to have superhuman abilities. The soldier in the play belies these perceptions. Apart from the fact of his comical appearance, we know that his capture has been the result of his own inexperience, or perhaps military incompetence.

His arrival signals a number of shifts in our perceptions of the other characters who we come to see in terms of their reactions to the prisoner. Bamforth's humanity becomes apparent, as does Mitchem's ruthlessness; Whitaker's stupidity and ineptness is confirmed, as is Macleish's moral uncertainty. The Japanese soldier has no dialogue and perhaps because of this the audience is able to see him as representative of all soldiers. We learn that he has a family, including a baby; he is willing to share his cigarettes; he is keen to please and, above all, he is afraid. The Japanese soldier's ordinariness enables us to equate him with the members of the patrol. Like them, we feel, he is simply one of 'The Long and the Short and the Tall'.

MINOR CHARACTERS

WHITAKER

Incompetent
Afraid
Pathetic

Inept and very frightened, Whitaker is a minor character who serves a number of important purposes in the play. He resembles the Japanese soldier in that he too collects enemy souvenirs, and perhaps also in his general ineptitude. He is very young, which might account for his nervousness and general incompetence. The details we learn of his home life – he is from Newcastle, he was stationed at Catterick, he has a girlfriend who has not written to him for some time – serve to emphasise his inexperience and his youthfulness.

Whitaker's incompetence adds to the realism of the play in the same way that the faulty radio does. This, Willis Hall seems to be saying, is the reality of the conscripted British army, unglamorous and sometimes bungling. The fact that Whitaker collects Japanese souvenirs enables Bamforth to argue successfully against the prisoner's accusers over the British cigarette case. Again, at the end of the play, it is Whitaker's ineptitude in accidentally shooting the prisoner that enables the Japanese to locate the patrol's whereabouts. In the aftermath of the attack, with his last breath, Whitaker calls for his mother. His death seems meaningless and, because he is so young, all the more poignant.

Smith

Level-headed
Family man
Essentially decent

Smith is another minor character about whom we learn a few telling details. He is slightly older than the rest of the conscripted men and, like the prisoner, is a husband and father. He lives in a council house with a small garden somewhere in the north of England. In civilian life he liked to listen to football on the wireless. As with the Japanese soldier, these few details serve to emphasise his ordinariness and his humanity. It is through conversation with Smith that we learn details of Whitaker's life back home. He is level-headed, able to deal with Bamforth's cheek and even to defend Whitaker against Bamforth's bullying. Like Macleish, he is unwilling to kill the prisoner when he is first captured. He is, it seems, a decent man whose ordinariness is underscored by his very name.

Nevertheless, Smith, again like Macleish, is willing ultimately to go along with the killing of the prisoner on the grounds that 'it's him or us'. When Bamforth calls on him to stand with him against the rest, Smith replies 'Don't ask me Bammo. Leave me out of it' (p. 83).

Evans

Weak physically
Weak in character
Duped by
Bamforth

The Welshman Evans acts alternately as the foil for and the butt of Bamforth's humour. Indeed Bamforth plays him like a musical instrument, cruelly mocking then cunningly flattering him to extort a cigarette. As with Smith and Whitaker, we learn some details about his peace-time life in Wales which make him seem unworldly and even naïve. In common with the other conscripts he has few soldierly qualities.

Though he tries to stand up to Bamforth, he is physically incapable of backing up his threats. The fact that he reads women's magazines sent from home by his mother, and that he has a girlfriend, the daughter of his mother's friend, adds to our impression of him as an ordinary man probably quite unsuited to being a soldier. Like Smith, he goes along with Mitchem's decision to kill the prisoner, arguing feebly 'You never know about that fag case, do you, son?' (p. 83).

LANGUAGE & STYLE

The Long and the Short and the Tall should be seen in the context of developments in the British theatre of the 1950s. The trend was towards **realism** (see Literary Terms) both in the subject-matter and in the language of drama. This was the era of **kitchen-sink drama** (see Literary Terms) when plays such as John Osborne's influential *Look Back In Anger* and Arnold Wesker's *Roots* were first produced. These plays were characterised by their portrayal of working-class or lower-middle-class life and by their domestic realism. The movement can be seen as a reaction by young playwrights against the **drawing-room comedies** (see Literary Terms) of the likes of Terence Rattigan and Noël Coward. *The Long and the Short and the Tall* is part of this new **genre** (see Literary Terms) because:

- the characters are working-class
- there is an attempt at **realism** (see Literary Terms) in the dialogue
- of the cynicism in the attitudes of the characters

THE CHARACTERS

Believable working-class 'types'?   Most of the characters are simply drawn. We rely upon the strength of the performances and the relationships between the actors to give the parts their vitality. Yet, even on the page, these characters ring true. The antagonisms between the men and their simple desire to survive contribute to the realism of the play. The few personal details we learn about the men emphasise their ordinariness. The tension of the play relies upon the sense of ordinary men faced with the prospect of killing a fellow human being.

The language, however, is realistic only within the legal constraints imposed upon the theatre of the day. Plays had to be submitted to the Lord Chamberlain's office where they were vetted for, among other things, obscenity. For that reason there is little profanity in the play and there is no use of the more common expletives although Bamforth uses the **euphemism** (see Literary Terms) 'Flipping' and asserts that 'All Corps are bastards' (p. 7), and Smith refers to 'Bloody southerners' (p. 6). Overall, the vocabulary of the dialogue is faithful to the everyday speech of working-class men.

Using his own experience

As a writer with a military background, Willis Hall was able to pepper his dialogue with the slang of the British army. This includes borrowings from the native languages of the country in which the play was set, 'Move yourselves! Gillo! Lacas! Lacas!' (p. 2), which adds to the authenticity of the military setting and also gives us a sense of the men being in a closed world with its own language and values. At the same time, Willis Hall wished to emphasise that the British army was made up of different sorts of people from different parts of the country and used regional accents to do this when the play was originally performed in 1958. Indeed, it is the use of language that, to a very large degree, gives the play its realism and vitality.

TUDY SKILLS

PART FOUR

S TUDY SKILLS

H OW TO USE QUOTATIONS

One of the secrets of success in writing essays is the way you use quotations. There are five basic principles:
- Put inverted commas at the beginning and end of the quotation
- Write the quotation exactly as it appears in the original
- Do not use a quotation that repeats what you have just written
- Use the quotation so that it fits into your sentence
- Keep the quotation as short as possible

Quotations should be used to develop the line of thought in your essays.

Your comment should not duplicate what is in your quotation. For example:

Mitchem tells Macleish that war is a far more difficult business than is assumed by those who have not experienced it. He says, 'The trouble is with war – a lot of it's like this – most of it. Too much.'

Far more effective is to write:

Mitchem tells Macleish that 'The trouble is with war – a lot of it's like this – most of it. Too much.'

However, the most sophisticated way of using the writer's words is to embed them into your sentence:

Mitchem's experience has taught him to despise men like Macleish who 'like to come the greater glory of mankind'.

When you use quotations in this way, you are demonstrating the ability to use text as evidence to support your ideas - not simply including words from the original to prove you have read it.

Everyone writes differently. Work through the suggestions given here and adapt the advice to suit your own style and interests. This will improve your essay-writing skills and allow your personal voice to emerge.

The following points indicate in ascending order the skills of essay writing:

- Picking out one or two facts about the story and adding the odd detail
- Writing about the text by retelling the story
- Retelling the story and adding a quotation here and there
- Organising an answer which explains what is happening in the text and giving quotations to support what you write

....

- Writing in such a way as to show that you have thought about the intentions of the writer of the text and that you understand the techniques used
- Writing at some length, giving your viewpoint on the text and commenting by picking out details to support your views
- Looking at the text as a work of art, demonstrating clear critical judgement and explaining to the reader of your essay how the enjoyment of the text is assisted by literary devices, linguistic effects and psychological insights; showing how the text relates to the time when it was written

The dotted line above represents the division between lower and higher level grades. Higher-level performance begins when you start to consider your response as a reader of the text. The highest level is reached when you offer an enthusiastic personal response and show how this piece of literature is a product of its time.

Coursework essay

Set aside an hour or so at the start of your work to plan what you have to do.

- List all the points you feel are needed to cover the task. Collect page references of information and quotations that will support what you have to say. A helpful tool is the highlighter pen: this saves painstaking copying and enables you to target precisely what you want to use.
- Focus on what you consider to be the main points of the essay. Try to sum up your argument in a single sentence, which could be the closing sentence of your essay. Depending on the essay title, it could be a statement about a character: Mitchem's cold military logic constantly challenges the humanitarian sympathies of both the other characters and the audience; an opinion about setting: The tin miners' hut provides a claustrophobic environment in which the tension between the characters intensifies; or a judgement on a theme: The principal theme of the play is the morality of killing a fellow human being. Each character is defined by his response to this dilemma.
- Make a short essay plan. Use the first paragraph to introduce the argument you wish to make. In the following paragraphs develop this argument with details, examples and other possible points of view. Sum up your argument in the last paragraph. Check you have answered the question.
- Write the essay, remembering all the time the central point you are making.
- On completion, go back over what you have written to eliminate careless errors and improve expression. Read it aloud to yourself, or, if you are feeling more confident, to a relative or friend.

If you can, try to type your essay, using a word processor. This will allow you to correct and improve your writing without spoiling its appearance.

Examination essay

The essay written in an examination often carries more marks than the coursework essay even though it is written under considerable time pressure.

In the revision period build up notes on various aspects of the text you are using. Fortunately, in acquiring this set of York Notes on *The Long and the Short and the Tall,* you have made a prudent beginning! York Notes are set out to give you vital information and help you to construct your personal overview of the text.

Make notes with appropriate quotations about the key issues of the set text. Go into the examination knowing your text and having a clear set of opinions about it.

In most English Literature examinations you can take in copies of your set books. This in an enormous advantage although it may lull you into a false sense of security. Beware! There is simply not enough time in an examination to read the book from scratch.

In the examination

- Read the question paper carefully and remind yourself what you have to do.
- Look at the questions on your set texts to select the one that most interests you and mentally work out the points you wish to stress.
- Remind yourself of the time available and how you are going to use it.
- Briefly map out a short plan in note form that will keep your writing on track and illustrate the key argument you want to make.
- Then set about writing it.
- When you have finished, check through to eliminate errors.

To summarise, these are the keys to success:

- **Know the text**
- **Have a clear understanding of and opinions on the storyline, characters, setting, themes and writer's concerns**
- **Select the right material**
- **Plan and write a clear response, continually bearing the question in mind**

A typical essay question on *The Long and the Short and the Tall* is followed by a sample essay plan in note form. This does not present the only answer to the question, merely one answer. Do not be afraid to include your own ideas and leave out some of the ones in this sample! Remember that quotations are essential to prove and illustrate the points you make.

In what ways do Mitchem and Bamforth differ and what do they have in common?

A question like this anticipates a wide-ranging response. These two members of the patrol are, after all, the play's principal characters. It is largely through them that the playwright discusses the morality of war and the killing of other human beings.

An outline of an essay in response to the question might look like this:

Part 1:
Introduction
Mitchem is a professional soldier who has experienced warfare. Bamforth is essentially a civilian in uniform, in many ways unsuited to military life.

Part 2:
Their attitudes towards military discipline
Bamforth is the typical 'barrack-room lawyer', describe his confrontations with authority figures. Mitchem is leader of the patrol yet is prepared to bend the rules in order to get the job done. Describe how this is evident in the early part of the play.

Part 3:
Their attitudes towards war
Bamforth is completely cynical. Describe how he plans to escape if the enemy arrives. Give examples of his sarcasm aimed at the army. Give examples of what might be interpreted as his naïvety (his protection of the prisoner). Describe Mitchem's cynicism about war – evident in his conversation with Macleish in Act II.

Part 4:
Their attitude towards the Japanese soldier
Describe how their initial attitude towards the prisoner differs. Mitchem prevents Bamforth from killing him. Explain why Mitchem changes his mind about what to do with the prisoner. Describe Bamforth's changing

relationship with the prisoner and why he decides to defy Mitchem's orders at the climax of the play.

Part 5:
Conclusion

There are more similarities between the two men than might be at first apparent. They are both to some extent cynical about war. Bamforth disregards military discipline yet, because he is a 'barrack-room lawyer', is prepared to 'play it by the book' when it suits him. Mitchem, as a professional soldier, 'plays it by the book' yet is prepared to disregard the rules, as he does when he decides to kill the prisoner, in order to accomplish what he regards as a more important task. What separates the men, ultimately, is Mitchem's experience.

FURTHER QUESTIONS

Make a plan as shown and attempt these quaestions.

1 Why do you think the author called the play *The Long and the Short and the Tall*?
2 Why do you think Bamforth's attitude towards the prisoner changes as the play progresses?
3 How do Mitchem's decisions contribute to the ultimate fate of the patrol, and would things have turned out differently had Johnstone been in command?
4 How do the conscripted men react to the dangerous situation in which they find themselves?
5 What impression does the play give of the British army as a whole?
6 What reasons do the men in the patrol have for behaving as they do towards the prisoner?
7 During the play we learn something about the backgrounds of Evans, Smith and Whitaker. How does this add to our understanding of the play?

8 What do we learn about Macleish during his conversations with Mitchem concerning the fate of the prisoner, and what do you think of him?

9 How do you account for the lasting appeal of this play?

10 Willis Hall has said that the play is 'about human dignity'. How far do you think this is true?

CULTURAL CONNECTIONS

BROADER PERSPECTIVES

Plays

A fascinating comparison can be made between *The Long and the Short and the Tall* and R.C. Sherriff's *Journey's End*. The latter is a play written about the playwright's experiences in the First World War (1914–18) and was first performed in the 1920s. It is written from the point of view of the officer class and the social attitudes are therefore different too. We see some cynicism in the play, but the dominant attitude towards war is one of stoicism.

There is an interesting contrast between the treatment of prisoners in the two plays. In *Journey's End* a captured German is treated with the utmost consideration despite his refusal to divulge information under interrogation. At no time do we feel that his life is at risk from his captors. Elsewhere in the play there are examples of acts of chivalry on the part of the Germans, holding fire while the British retrieve their dead and wounded, for instance. Contrast this with the fear, suspicion and evident loathing that exists between some of the men in *The Long and the Short and the Tall* and their Japanese enemy. Had attitudes changed in the years separating the two wars, or can the difference be explained in another way?

Both plays examine the behaviour of men under the pressure of war. Interestingly, in both we also see something of male attitudes towards women. In this case there is a similarity, for both portray war as the preserve of men and the characters' attitudes combine condescension and misogyny. In *Journey's End* the main character, Stanhope, feels unable to go home on leave because his fiancée does not understand the suffering he has endured and the changes it has brought about in his personality. Elsewhere in the play we hear of the 'tarts' who provide recreation for the drunken officers when on leave from the front. The important relationships in the play are male, forged through comradeship in battle and shared privation in the trenches. In *The Long and the Short and the Tall* we have Mitchem's stark testimony on the reasons why men join the army. He blames women. Bamforth gives voice to the fears of the ordinary soldier that, while they are away fighting, their women are prostituting themselves with their allies.

Books

Stephen Crane's classic novel, *The Red Badge of Courage*, set against the background of the American Civil War, examines the reaction of a young man to his first experience of combat. A child's view of the Second World War in the Far East is given in J.G. Ballard's *Empire of the Sun*.

George MacDonald Fraser's *Quartered Safe Out Here* is an account, both gripping and moving, of his experiences as a very young soldier taking part in the Allies, counter-attack against the Japanese in the Far East, launched in 1944, two years after the fall of Singapore and the events of this play.

Poetry

No study of attitudes towards warfare in this century would be complete without reference to the poetry of the First World War, particularly that of Wilfred Owen and Siegfried Sassoon. The shattering events of the war are harrowingly conveyed in the poems of men who lived, fought and, in many cases, died in the trenches of the Western Front.

It is interesting to compare the work of poets of the First World War with that of poets who experienced combat in the Second World War. We can see in the poems of men such as Keith Douglas and John Pudney a more ambivalent attitude towards war, one which can also be detected in Mitchem's speeches in *The Long and the Short and the Tall.* It is also interesting to note that much less poetry emerged from the experience of the Second World War than the First. Perhaps this is because the sense of disillusionment with war, and therefore the horror of it, was much greater for those who suffered during the earlier conflict. Certainly in the later play there is something of a weary acceptance of the need to fight despite what experience had taught.

Films

A film of the play was made in 1960 starring Laurence Harvey, Richard Todd and Richard Harris. With a screenplay adapted from the original text by Willis Hall, it captures all the tension and claustrophobia of the stage production. Although the play is written about the Second World War we must not forget that it was written and first performed thirteen years after the war had ended. The attitudes portrayed in plays and films produced during the war were quite different. For example, Laurence Olivier's *Henry V* (1944) is unapologetically patriotic in tone, reflecting film makers' acceptance of the need to maintain the morale and fighting spirit of audiences, both military and civilian. Postwar films such as *The Dambusters* (1954) and *The Battle of Britain* (1959) are straightforward celebrations of British victories during the war and offer little reflection on the moral implications of war in general. Their popularity as entertainment is evidence that a variety of opinions about war continue to exist. Later films, such as *The Deer Hunter* (1978), *Apocalypse Now* (1979) and *Platoon* (1986), although exploring aspects of the American involvement in the Vietnam War from an American point of view, in their own ways reflect the changes in attitudes towards war in the latter part of this century.

Music

The title of the play is taken from a popular song of the war years. This and other songs, popularised via sheet music, gramophone recordings, radio and music hall, captured the mood of the British people through six years of war. We can also see in the songs the subtle differences in attitudes towards the war. Flannigan and Allen's 'We're Going to Hang Out the Washing on the Siegfried Line' expressed a jaunty optimism about victory over the Germans, while Vera Lynn's 'The White Cliffs of Dover' and 'We'll Meet Again' looked forward to the end of the war and a return to normality. The power of music to inspire is very clearly demonstrated in the music William Walton composed for the aforementioned *Henry V* and his Spitfire music for the intensely patriotic film *The Battle of Britain*. And you do not need to see the films to know what attitudes they express, the music on its own does that very precisely.

LITERARY TERMS

climax a decisive moment in drama

cynicism distrust and contempt for the values of others and of accepted standards

denouement the final clarification or resolution of a plot in a play or other work of literature

drawing-room comedy drama that is mainly concerned with the lives of the English upper classes. For example the plays of Terence Rattigan, such as *French Without Tears* (1937), and Noël Coward's *Private Lives* (1933) and *Blithe Spirit* (1941)

euphemism an inoffensive word substituted for one that is considered offensive

genre a type of literature, for instance poetry, drama, biography, fiction

ironic/irony when what is said or written is the opposite to what is meant, or when there is a great difference between what is expected and what happens

kitchen-sink drama drama which portrays working-class or lower-middle-class life, with an emphasis on domestic realism. Examples include *A Taste of Honey* written by Shelagh Delaney at the age of 17, and Arnold Wesker's *Chicken Soup With Barley* (1958), *Roots* (1959) and *I'm Talking about Jerusalem* (1960), the three now collectively known as 'the Wesker Trilogy'. These plays can be seen as a reaction against the drawing-room comedies of Terence Rattigan and Noël Coward

moral relativism the theory that morals are not absolute but are relative to a person's nature and situation

paradox a self-contradictory situation or statement

realism an accurate representation of things as they 'really' are in 'ordinary' life

tension a sense of unease, trepidation or expectation

TEST ANSWERS

TEST YOURSELF (Act I Part 1 – pages 1–27)

A 1 Johnstone *(page 3)*
... 2 Mitchem *(page 3)*
   3 Bamforth *(page 5)*
   4 Macleish *(page 7)*
   5 Smith *(page 16)*
   6 Smith *(page 6)*
   7 Whitaker *(page 18)*
   8 Macleish *(page 25)*

TEST YOURSELF (Act 1 Part 1 – pages 28–50)

A 1 Johnstone *(page 29)*
... 2 Mitchem *(page 32)*
   3 Smith *(page 36)*
   4 Macleish *(page 39)*

   5 Johnstone *(page 43)*
   6 Smith *(page 47)*
   7 The prisoner *(page 34)*
   8 Bamforth *(page 46)*

TEST YOURSELF (Act II)

A 1 Whitaker *(page 52)*
... 2 Macleish *(page 53)*
   3 Mitchem *(page 54)*
   4 Bamforth *(page 63)*
   5 Johnstone *(page 65)*
   6 Macleish *(page 67)*
   7 Whitaker *(page 75)*
   8 Bamforth *(page 78)*

Notes

York Notes – the Ultimate Literature Guides

York Notes are recognised as the best literature study guides.
If you have enjoyed using this book and have found it useful, you
can now order others directly from us – simply follow the ordering
instructions below.

HOW TO ORDER

Decide which title(s) you require and then order in one of the following
ways:

Booksellers
All titles available from good bookstores.

By post
List the title(s) you require in the space provided overleaf,
select your method of payment, complete your name and
address details and return your completed order form and
payment to:

> *Addison Wesley Longman Ltd*
> *PO BOX 88*
> *Harlow*
> *Essex CM19 5SR*

By phone
Call our Customer Information Centre on 01279 623923 to
place your order, quoting mail number: HEYN1.

By fax
Complete the order form overleaf, ensuring you fill in your
name and address details and method of payment, and fax it
to us on 01279 414130.

By e-mail
E-mail your order to us on awlhe.orders@awl.co.uk listing
title(s) and quantity required and providing full name and
address details as requested overleaf. Please quote mail
number: HEYN1. Please do not send credit card details by
e-mail.

York Notes Order Form

Titles required:

Quantity	Title/ISBN	Price

Sub total _____

Please add £2.50 postage & packing _____

(*P & P is free for orders over £50*) _____

Total _____

Mail no: HEYN1

Your Name _____

Your Address _____

_____

Postcode _____ Telephone _____

Method of payment

☐ I enclose a cheque or a P/O for £_____ made payable to Addison Wesley Longman Ltd

☐ Please charge my Visa/Access/AMEX/Diners Club card
Number _____ Expiry Date _____
Signature _____ Date _____

(please ensure that the address given above is the same as for your credit card)

Prices and other details are correct at time of going to press but may change without notice. All orders are subject to status.

☐ *Please tick this box if you would like a complete listing of Longman Study Guides (suitable for GCSE and A-level students)*

York Press

Longman

Addison Wesley Longman